Billibonk
& the Big Itch

Billibonk
& the
Big Itch

by
Philip Ramsey

illustrated by
Robin Runci Mazo

Pegasus Communications, Inc.   Waltham

Billibonk and the Big Itch by Philip Ramsey
Copyright © 1998 by Philip Ramsey
Art © Pegasus Communications, Inc.

Library of Congress Cataloging-in-Publication Data
Ramsey, Philip.
Billibonk and the big itch / Philip Ramsey; illustrated by Robin Runci
Mazo
ISBN 1-883823-17-X (softcover)
1. Jungle animals—Fiction. 2. Problem solving—Fiction. 3. Fables,
International.
I. Mazo, Robin Runci. II. Title.
PS3568.A4715B55 1997
813'54—dc21 97-24972

CIP

Acquiring editor: Kellie Wardman O'Reilly
Project editor: Lauren Johnson
Design: Robert Lowe
Production: Dartmouth Publishing, Inc.

♻ Printed on recycled paper.
Printed in the United States of America.
First printing August 1997.

Pegasus Communications, Inc.
One Moody Street
Waltham, MA 02154-5339

www.pegasuscom.com

To my fabulous wife, Debbie

Contents

PART THREE

PART FOUR

PART ONE

1

Trees Cracking

S THE SUN RISES EACH MORNING, the jungle of Knith becomes a noisy, bustling place. Throughout the jungle, birds sing and squawk, signaling to all the daytime animals that it is time to wake up.

All the chattering and screeching of the birds jolted Billibonk the elephant wide awake, and he lumbered to his feet stiffly. He had spent a restless evening. His whole back had itched all night long, and he had tossed and turned before finally falling asleep just before dawn. He muttered irritably to himself and sidled his way up to a medium-sized tree, where he began rubbing his back briskly against the rough bark.

"Ahhhh," he sighed, as the itching subsided. "That's better."

But as Billibonk scratched his back against the tree, he leaned a little too hard. "Crack!" went the tree. It slowly began to topple over. Loud cries of "Hey, elephant!" and "What's going on?!" rang out as angry birds abandoned their perches in a swirl of feathers.

Seeing the mess he had caused and feeling hugely embarrassed, Billibonk quickly trotted away to find his herd. Other elephants, he reassured himself, understand how easy it is to knock down a tree accidentally. "Elephants don't give you a hard time about little things like trees," he said grumpily to himself, "not like those birds."

As he came into a clearing, he heard another loud "Crack!" Ahead

of him, another tree was falling, and more birds were yelling out their protests. This time it was Jawoody, the most senior member of the elephant herd, who looked shame-faced. "Whoops!" she said. "I guess I pushed a little too hard scratching my back."

"Could have happened to anyone," Billibonk said. "Is your back itching, too?"

"It sure is," Jawoody rumbled. "I've never felt anything like it!"

"Funny how we're both getting itchy at the same time," Billibonk said thoughtfully. "Though I've noticed that my itch has been getting worse and worse over the last few days."

"Probably just a coincidence," Jawoody said, dismissing Billibonk's comment with a shake of her massive head.

"I don't know . . . ," Billibonk responded. "Let's see if the others are itching, too."

Jawoody and Billibonk set out through the forest looking for the rest of their herd. It didn't take them long to find out that several other elephants had also slept badly and had woken up itching. The more the group talked about the itch, the more all the elephants felt the urge to scratch.

"This is your fault, Billibonk," Cody said. Although Cody was Billibonk's best friend, he sounded quite unfriendly at the moment. "You had this itch first, so you must have passed it on to all of us!" 🐾

"That's not fair!" Billibonk protested. "I haven't done anything except get itchy!" But no one seemed to believe him. In fact, he noticed that the others had all begun to look at him accusingly.

It was clear to Billibonk that he had a problem, and that he needed to spend some time thinking about it. He knew that he often needed help to think

> 🐾 **Often when elephants don't understand why something bad is happening, they try to explain it by looking for someone else to blame.**

through his problems, so he decided to look for his friend Frankl the mouse. "I'm not standing around here just to be called an itch-carrier," he huffed as he turned and trotted away.

"I'm glad he's going," Cody said ungraciously. "Maybe now my back will stop itching." Just then, the tree he was rubbing against gave a sharp "Crack!" A branch tumbled down, hitting Cody on the end of his trunk—the most sensitive part of any elephant. "Ow!" he cried. "That Billibonk—he's *really* making me mad now!"

2

Using "Whys"

WORD HAD SPREAD QUICKLY through the jungle that the elephant herd was acting strangely. So, Frankl the mouse was not surprised to see Billibonk show up outside the thorn patch that was home to him and many other mice. Frankl smiled with pleasure at the sight of his old friend; he enjoyed Billibonk's company and their adventures together.

"Hey elephant!" Frankl shouted. (Frankl was so tiny compared to Billibonk that he often had to yell so the elephant could hear him). "What's with all the tree-smashing?"

"Oh, Frankl," Billibonk said. "We're not *trying* to smash the trees! The elephants all have a bad itch, and when we scratch ourselves on the trees, sometimes the trees fall down. I was hoping *you* could help us with the problem." It often amazed Billibonk that someone like a mouse, with such a small body, could have so many big and clever ideas. Like most elephants, Billibonk had grown up thinking that the size of an animal's *body* was what mattered most. Since coming to know Frankl, though, he had begun to realize that the size of an animal's *ideas* were just as important—maybe even more so.

At the moment, though, Billibonk wasn't thinking much about thinking, he was thinking about his itching problem. "This itching is driving me crazy, Frankl. How can I make it stop?"

"Before we think about how to solve your problem," Frankl said, "we'd better find out what's making you itchy in the first place. Have you ever been itchy like this before?"

"Sure," Billibonk said. "Elephants are always getting itchy, but never like this. Usually an itch gets a little bit annoying, then it goes away. This itch just keeps getting worse. Do you think maybe I should roll in those thorns to help scratch it?"

"No!" Frankl said. (He lived in those very thorns!) He quickly suggested another plan. "I think you need to learn about using 'whys' to solve problems. My grandfather used to tell me that *'whys'* make you *wise*."

"I don't understand," Billibonk said impatiently. "How will 'whys' stop my itching?"

"We need to find out the *reasons* for your problem," Frankl explained. "The better we do that, the better we'll be able to fix things. Asking 'why' is one thing we can do. We also have to make sure to do it properly."

"Maybe we could start now?" Billibonk suggested, trying hard to look patient.

"OK," Frankl said. "It's time for our first 'why.'"

3

Bugs

"SO," FRANKL SAID, "let's start with, Why are you itching? To answer this first 'why,' I need to take a closer look at the problem. Do you mind if I climb on your back?"

"Not at all," Billibonk replied. "While you're there," he added hopefully, "maybe you could do a little scratching." Billibonk grasped Frankl gently with the tip of his trunk, lifted the mouse over his head, and deposited him on the very top of his broad back.

"Wow!" Frankl said. "You should see *this!*"

"What?! What?!" Billibonk blurted out.

"Well," Frankl said, "there are hundreds of bugs up here, and it looks like they're biting you. They're *everywhere!*"

"Ugh!" Billibonk said, shuddering so hard that Frankl almost fell off his back. The thought of that many bugs was quite disgusting. But Billibonk recovered and said, "Well, at least now we know what's making me itch. All we have to do is get rid of the bugs to solve my problem."

"Well . . . it's not that simple," Frankl said. "We've asked 'why' just once. We have to do better than that if we're going to get you fixed."

"But why can't you just start kicking those bugs off me?" Billibonk asked with an alarmed look on his face.

"Bugs have baby bugs," Frankl explained. "Even if I kick them off

one end of you, the bugs at the other end of you will be having babies. We mice know about these things, believe me. In my experience, the smaller the creature, the faster they make babies, and these bugs are pretty small. I bet they'd make new bug babies a lot faster than I could kick them off you. Hey!—Watch it!"

Billibonk had nervously begun rubbing up against a nearby, low-hanging branch, and once again Frankl clung to his back to keep from falling off. "Sorry, Frankl," Billibonk apologized. "These bugs have really got me upset. What should I *do*?" he pleaded.

"If we still don't know what to do, it must be time to ask 'why' again," Frankl said. "Why are there so many bugs on the elephants these days?"

"Maybe the bugs have just flown into the jungle," Billibonk suggested.

"Or perhaps you've always had a few on you, and now for some reason they're making more babies than usual," Frankl added.

"Maybe . . . ," Billibonk said distractedly. "Frankl, think of something *quick*—I just can't concentrate with all this itching!"

4

"Buts"

BILLIBONK," FRANKL ASKED HOPEFULLY, "tell me . . . have you noticed anything different about your back lately?" 🐾

"Frankl," his friend replied testily, "I've noticed that it has been very itchy!"

Frankl sighed. "Look, I'm trying to *help* you. Have you noticed anything besides the itch?"

"Nothing I can think of," Billibonk said. Frankl thought to himself that his friend's answer had come a little too quickly.

"Are there any elephants who *aren't* itchy?" Frankl asked.

"I'm sure there are," Billibonk answered. "But what do *they* have to do

> 🐾 Frankl knew that elephants often pay little attention to what's going on around them. Because they're so big, elephants don't have to worry so much about sudden dangers, the way mice do, so they don't feel the need to keep watch all the time.

with the problem?" He stamped his feet impatiently.

Frankl decided he was tired of doing all the thinking by himself and that the best way to help his friend concentrate was to be stern. "Billibonk!" he shouted, even more loudly than usual. "One of the things I've always liked about you is the way you know how to listen and learn.

Since you started itching, though, your listening has gone bad. You've started saying 'but' to *everything* I say!"

As you can imagine, elephants are not used to being scolded by mice. Billibonk started sputtering, "But . . .!" when he realized that Frankl was right. "Oh," he said, correcting himself. "What's so bad about 'but'?"

"The problem with 'buts,'" Frankl began, "is that they ruin a good conversation." Billibonk furrowed his brow, trying to understand. "Conversations are really wonderful things," Frankl continued. "When we talk together, we can have a good time *and* figure out the answers to our problems . . . like how to stop an elephant from itching."

"How do 'buts' ruin a conversation, then?" Billibonk asked.

"Well," Frankl replied, "a conversation has a kind of flow, like an elephant running." Billibonk nodded, thinking of times when he had enjoyed running through the jungle. "It takes a little while to work up some speed," Frankl continued, "then after a while, running—and conversing—gets easier. When a 'but' comes into a conversation, it stops the ideas from flowing in one direction. The ideas have to find another direction to go. The conversation starts and stops and never builds up any speed."

"Well, if getting rid of 'buts' helps me get rid of bugs, then I'll try," Billibonk said, fanning his itching side with one huge ear.

"Good!" Frankl said. 🐾 "Now let's go and find an elephant who's not itching." Frankl scrambled along Billibonk's backbone and found a perch on top of the elephant's great head, and the pair set off to look for the herd.

🐾 Frankl knew that "but" can be a very useful word. When Billibonk used it, though, he was blocking the conversation. Frankl wanted to help his friend avoid getting into the "but" habit.

5

No "Buts"

A S BILLIBONK TROTTED THROUGH THE JUNGLE, Frankl clung to the hairs atop the elephant's head. Between bounces, Frankl told Billibonk why it was taking so long to decide how to fix the itching problem.

"You see," Frankl said, "your itching isn't the problem—it's just a *sign* that there's a problem that needs fixing. In one way, your itching is good: The more you itch, the more you want to fix the *real* problem that's causing the itch."

"You're right about that," Billibonk huffed.

"We *could* find a way to make the itching stop, but that wouldn't fix the real problem. When you rub up against a tree, the scratching makes the itch go away. The itch comes back right away, though, because you haven't fixed the real problem."

"So . . ." Billibonk said gloomily, "I have to put up with the itch while we find out what the real problem is and fix it?"

Frankl reached forward and patted Billibonk's forehead. "Yes!" he said encouragingly. "You have to be brave about it. Scratching feels good; it feels like you're doing something useful. In fact, I bet most of the herd are so busy rubbing against trees that they're not even thinking about looking for a real solution. But *we're* going to solve the problem our own way. We're going to keep asking 'why' until we find the real problem. Then we can figure out what to do about it."

Frankl settled more comfortably into his perch on Billibonk's head; he was getting used to the bouncing as the elephant trotted along. "So far," Frankl continued, "we've asked 'why' twice. The first time, it helped us find the bugs. Now we want to know why there are so *many* bugs all of a sudden. To answer this question, we need to find elephants who *don't* have the bugs, and figure out what makes them different. Make sense?"

"I think so," Billibonk puffed, "but—OW! You bit my ear!"

"That's my way of helping you to stop saying 'but.'"

"But—OW! Oh, all right. Tell me how to stop saying it, then."

Frankl grinned and said, "One good way to stop saying 'but' is to ask me to explain what I'm saying. Or, you could give your own opinion. You could say something like: 'I think so. One thing I don't understand is such-and-such.'"

"I get it!" Billibonk said excitedly. "It's going to take practice, though." He took a deep breath and said, "Let's start over—ask me again if our plan makes sense."

"OK," Frankl said. "Here goes: Does all that make sense?"

"I think so," Billibonk said carefully. "What worries me about my problem is that we could be asking 'why' forever while I just keep on itching. How often do we have to ask it?"

"That was great!" Frankl said, pleased with his friend's progress. "You're a fast learner!"

"Thanks!" Billibonk said happily. "So, what's the answer?"

"Oh. Well, usually by the time I've asked 'why' five times, I've got a good idea of what the real problem is. Or, we could ask 'why' until we can no longer do anything about the answers we discover."

"Hmmm . . ." Billibonk murmured doubtfully. A loud "Crack!" suddenly rang out in the distance.

"What was that?!" Frankl asked, startled.

Billibonk knew the sound all too well. "That's another tree that couldn't stand up to someone's scratching," he replied.

They hurried on to find the herd.

Frankl Explains:

Why scratching doesn't solve the itching problem

Even though scratching might help for a little while . . .

unless you fix what
is really causing
the problem . . .

the problem will
keep coming back.

PART TWO

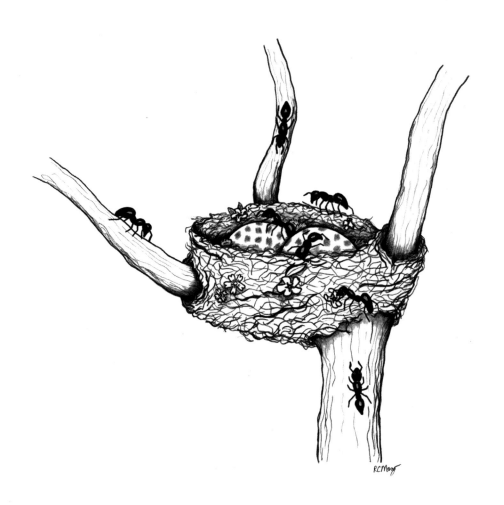

6

Honka's Theory

BILLIBONK AND FRANKL FINALLY ARRIVED at the shady clearing where the elephants often relaxed during the heat of the day. They stopped in their tracks, and blinked in amazement, when they saw the mess the itching herd had made. The area was littered with broken branches and tree trunks. One frantic elephant wiggled on the ground with his feet in the air. There were deep holes in the soil where other elephants had thrown themselves down to relieve their itching. The air swirled with the dust that the flailing animals had churned up.

"Wow," Frankl said to himself. "These elephants really need help."

Billibonk tried to ask which elephants were itching and which weren't, but the herd was in too bad a mood to cooperate. Once again, Cody blamed Billibonk. "This is all your fault!" he snarled.

Suddenly, Frankl spied a large gray shape slumped beneath a tree across the clearing. He tapped Billibonk's head and pointed. "What's that?" he asked.

Billibonk's eyes grew wide with shock. "It's Honka!" he said. "Those bugs have bitten him to death! Yuck—the birds are already pecking at his body!"

As Frankl clutched the top of Billibonk's head and held on with all his might, Billibonk charged over to investigate. Two brown birds that had been standing on Honka's back flew into some over-hanging branches just in time to avoid being trampled.

Billibonk looked sadly down at his herd mate. As he lowered his head to examine Honka more closely, Honka suddenly snorted, yawned, and opened his eyes! "What's all the ruckus, Billibonk?" Honka asked irritably. "Every time I try to get some sleep around here, someone pushes a tree down on top of me. Let me sleep, will you?!"

> 🐾 Elephants are proud of their size and weight. They get easily offended if someone suggests that they have some of the same problems as smaller animals.

"Sorry, Honka," Billibonk said. "We thought you were . . . oh, never mind. Anyway, you don't seem as itchy as the other elephants."

"No, I'm not itchy. Itching is for light-weights," Honka said. 🐾

"Well, some of us have a really bad itch," Billibonk explained. "How come you don't seem to have the problem?"

"I was thinking about this over breakfast," Honka responded, "and I've decided that I don't itch because I'm the biggest elephant in the herd. It stands to reason, doesn't it?" 🐾

> 🐾 When an elephant doesn't really know why something good has happened to him and not to others, he will often decide it must be something special about him that caused the good thing.

Billibonk hesitated. "Do you think bugs might have something to do with you not itching?" he asked.

"Bugs? No—it's all about size. If you ever get to be my size, you won't have to worry about itching."

"Hmmm . . . ," Billibonk said. Honka settled back down against the tree and closed his eyes, and Billibonk wandered away some distance so he could talk privately with Frankl. "What do you think, mouse?" Billibonk whispered to Frankl.

"I think he's just guessing," Frankl said. "After all, he doesn't know about the bugs."

"He *is* the biggest, though," Billibonk said. "Maybe he's right about size having something to do with it."

"You *all* look huge to *me*," Frankl chuckled. "I'll tell you what: I'll climb on Honka's back while he's sleeping and see if I can find some clues." With that, Frankl scurried down Billibonk's trunk and headed for Honka.

7

Birds

FRANKL SCAMPERED UP onto Honka's back without waking the giant elephant. Immediately, he noticed how few bugs there were on Honka. He did find some, though, but he decided that they were probably the usual amount. "Why are there so many more bugs on the other elephants?" he wondered.

His thinking was interrupted by the sound of flapping wings. One of the birds that had been sitting on Honka before had come back and settled on Honka's large haunch. "Look out, mouse," the bird squawked. "Don't touch bugs. Find own elephant." ꞷ

> ꞷ Birds have great trouble forming words, because they don't have lips and teeth. So, they don't bother with words that aren't necessary for getting their point across.

"OK, bird," Frankl said. He watched as the bird snapped up three bugs and gulped them down one right after the other. "My name's Frankl, by the way."

"Hi Frankl. I'm Rork. Excuse me." The bird snatched up two more bugs. This time, instead of swallowing them, he held them in his beak and flew off.

"Well, well," thought Frankl. "That's what happens to the bugs. I bet the elephants never even notice birds on their backs. For some reason, this bird is eating bugs off Honka, and not off the other elephants."

Frankl's thoughts were interrupted once again as Rork returned and landed on Honka with a burst of wing-flapping. The bird grabbed up several more bugs. "Do you mind if we talk for a while, Rork?" Frankl asked.

"Sure, Frankl. Soon. First I take hairs to Ella," the bird answered.

"Who's Ella?" Frankl asked. "And what do you mean by 'take hairs'?"

"Ella is mate," Rork replied. He swooped down to Honka's tail, grabbed two long hairs from the tuft on the end, and jerked them out. Honka twitched a little but kept sleeping. Rork flew off into the treetops.

"This is getting fascinating," Frankl murmured to himself. His mind raced as he waited for Rork to return. "I've answered the second 'why,'" Frankl said. "There are too many bugs on the other elephants because the birds aren't eating them. Why aren't they eating bugs from *all* the elephants? Why only Honka's bugs? This must be the next 'why.'"

Soon the bird returned once again. "What you want know, mouse?" he squawked.

"Rork, how come you took those hairs from Honka's tail? What are they for?"

"Nest-making time. Soon eggs, then chicks. Busy time."

"I'm sure it is. How do you use the hairs?"

"Hairs hold nest together," the bird replied, rolling his eyes as though this was something everyone should know. His gaze came to rest on a passing bug, which he snapped up in his beak and gulped down.

"There don't seem to be many bugs on this elephant," Frankl pointed out.

Rork cocked his head to one side. "About usual. Soon lots more."

"Oh? Why is that?"

"Didn't I say? New chick time. Always lots of bugs at new chick time. Need lots of bugs to feed chicks."

"I get it," Frankl said suddenly. "When you and your mate have your chicks, you'll be eating lots and lots of bugs!"

"We eat some, chicks eat most," Rork explained.

"Will you get them off *all* the elephants?"

"No. Plenty on this elephant for Rork and Ella."

"What about the bugs on the other elephants?" Frankl asked.

"We not greedy. Leave for other birds. Besides, each bird family has own elephant."

"But there aren't birds on the other elephants," Frankl pointed out. "You and Ella are the only bug-birds around."

Rork shrugged. "Lots of birds last chick time. Others go. Not come back. Too bad! More fun with lots of birds. See you later. Mate needs bugs." Rork grabbed three more bugs and flapped his way into the air once again.

Frankl watched him go. "Wait 'til Billibonk hears about this," he thought.

8

"Where Next?"

FRANKL SAW BILLIBONK deep in conversation with the other elephants in the clearing. Sure enough, not one of them had a bug-bird on its back. The elephants were still scratching their itchy skin on any surface they could find, so Frankl looked around for some way to climb to a position where he could get Billibonk's attention.

Scrambling onto a rock beside Billibonk, Frankl yelled, "Hey, elephant!" until his friend turned and saw him.

"Hey Frankl," Billibonk greeted him. "Did you find out anything?"

Frankl excitedly explained what he had learned about the birds and the time of year.

"You mean, this is the time of year when bugs are having lots of babies, and it just so happens that this is also the time when bug-birds are the most hungry?" Billibonk asked incredulously. "That's amazing!"

"I suppose so," Frankl said, though he was used to coincidences like this and was not quite so amazed. "We need to find out why the other bug-birds left. I'm convinced that the itching problem has something to do with birds. We need fewer bugs. To get fewer bugs, we need more birds. If we get more birds, they might leave like the other ones, unless we know what made them leave in the first place. I wonder why they flew away."

"Can't we just ask the birds?" Billibonk suggested, wondering why the mouse had not thought of this himself.

"I don't know," Frankl replied. "The way Rork spoke, he didn't seem like much of a thinker."

"What do you mean?" Billibonk asked.

"Well, he left words out when he spoke," Frankl explained.

"We'll only know if we ask him," Billibonk pointed out, and Frankl had to agree. "Let's find Honka and his birds," Billibonk said.

"*Honka's* birds?" Frankl laughed. "Rork and Ella would probably say that Honka was *their* elephant!"

The two chuckled and headed back to Honka, Frankl once more perched on Billibonk's head. They found the huge elephant exactly where they had left him, awake now and leisurely chomping on grass and leaves. "Hi, Billibonk!" Honka said through a mouthful. "Would you like a feed? You're looking a little skinny!"

"Don't mind if I do," Billibonk said, and he gratefully accepted a bundle of grass.

Frankl called over to Rork, who was stalking bugs on Honka's back. "Hey, bird! Hop over here for a minute. I want to talk with you."

When Rork landed on Billibonk's back, his eyes boggled at the sight of so many bugs. "Hang on, mouse," he said. "I get mate. She want talk, too, and then both eat bugs." And off he fluttered.

9

Ants

UST AS FRANKL EXPECTED, Rork and Ella returned immediately, settled down on Billibonk's back, and began snapping up the bountiful bugs. "So many," Ella croaked. "Some other birds need?"

"No," Frankl assured her. "You're the only two birds in the jungle eating these bugs. That's what I want to talk with you about—have you noticed that the elephants are acting strangely?"

"Yes," the two birds answered in unison. "Keep smashing trees, roll on ground," Ella said. Rork rolled his eyes and squawked, "Strange, strange."

"Our elephant—the big one—*he* not smash trees." Frankl smiled at the way Rork called Honka "our" elephant.

"We build nest in tree," Ella continued. "Lay two beautiful eggs. Elephants smash tree down. Have to start again. New nest in bigger tree. New eggs."

"Ella not happy unless got nest, got eggs, now chick time," Rork explained. Frankl nodded, delighted that the birds were talking so freely. He also felt sure that Billibonk appreciated the birds' eating bugs off his back.

"The reason they smash trees is they got lots bugs," Frankl said.

"Too many bugs. Make elephants itchy—scratch on trees. Elephants big and clumsy—smash trees." Billibonk, listening in on the conversation as he munched, snorted to let Frankl know he could hear. Frankl continued, "Not enough birds for all these elephants."

Without thinking about it, Frankl had begun talking like Rork and Ella.

"No," Rork said. "Birds go last year."

"Birds go?" Frankl asked, his ears perking up. "Why?"

"Ants!" Ella announced.

"Ants?" Frankl said. "What about the ants?"

"Last year," Ella began, "birds all make nests. Lay eggs. Then ants come. Take over nests. Eggs hatch, ants all over chicks. Yuck."

"Soon as chicks big enough," Rork continued. "Bird families go. Hate ants, leave jungle to get away. Go find new jungle."

"Why didn't *you* go?" Frankl asked.

"No ants in our nest," Rork answered promptly. "We like this jungle. Good elephants. Good bugs."

Frankl thought to himself, "It's time for the fourth 'why.'" He asked the birds, "Why do you think the ants took over the other birds' nests and not yours?"

"Stupid birds—warned them," Ella said. In the background, Rork echoed, "Stupid, stupid, stupid." Ella continued, "Other birds change nests. Not use elephant hairs. Tie nests with herbs instead. Make pretty."

"Your nests are made out of elephant hairs?" Frankl asked.

"No, no." Ella explained. "Make nest from grass. Tie grass *together* with hairs. Lots of grass, and some hairs. Other birds found long, stringy herbs—look like hairs. Use them instead."

"Why did the other birds stop using elephant hairs?" Frankl wondered.

"Smelly—what expect from elephant tail?" Rork said. Frankl grinned as he felt Billibonk stamp and snort under him at the insult.

Ella gulped down another bug and said, "Others want to make nests prettier. Stupid to change nests. Birds always use elephant hair. Anyway, ants like flowers and herbs."

"So," Frankl said, "you were the only birds who stayed, because you were the only ones still using the elephant hairs. Did you have any chicks last year?"

"Yes, yes," Rork nodded. "Two boy chicks. Not stay. Went to find mates. No mates here. Look somewhere else."

Ella looked sharply at Rork. "Stop eating," she ordered. "Build nest time. Come on. Eggs soon."

As the two birds flew off, Billibonk lifted his head to watch them.

"Well, well," Frankl said. "This is getting very interesting!"

10

Math

"WELL," BILLIBONK SNORTED. "I find all that bird-talk very hard to believe. Elephant hairs don't smell—what a bunch of nonsense!"

"Now don't go getting upset," Frankl said soothingly. "Let's think about what those birds said. When they say your hairs smell, I'm sure they mean it's just not the same as flowers. At least the smell doesn't attract ants," he said kindly.

Billibonk said "Harrumph!" and then added "So, we started out thinking there were too many bugs. Then we decided there weren't enough birds. Now it's too many ants. What next? I suppose we have to get rid of all the ants in the jungle."

"Oh no," Frankl replied. "Ants helped cause the problem, but they're not the problem anymore."

"I heard you say 'but,' Frankl," Billibonk pointed out.

"I thought I could get away with it," Frankl admitted. "I hope *you're* not thinking of biting *me*."

"Not *this* time," Billibonk teased, trying to sound stern. "Anyway, back to those ants—how come they're *not* the problem?"

"They were a problem for the birds who left the jungle," Frankl explained. "Rork and Ella are going to keep using elephant hair, so ants won't be a problem for *them*."

"If ants aren't the problem, then what should we do?" Billibonk asked.

"We don't have to do anything about ants, so we go back to the last 'why.' The problem is not enough birds."

"How can we fix that?"

"It will fix itself after a while. Rork and Ella will have a couple of chicks this year. Next year they'll have a couple more, plus their chicks will be grown up and will have chicks, too. Each year there'll be more and more birds, and after a while everything will be back to normal."

Billibonk shook his head as he tried to follow this line of reasoning. "'After a while,' you say—how long is that? There are twelve elephants in our herd—how long will we have to be itchy?"

"Well . . . I can't quite figure that out either," Frankl admitted. 🐾 "And what if their chicks this year can't find mates when they grow up?" Billibonk pointed out. "They'll leave like the others who left last year. That will mean another whole year of itching!"

"We have to find more birds from somewhere," Frankl said. "I suppose only bugbirds eat bugs."

"I don't know," Billibonk said. "Yesterday I didn't know that anything ate bugs."

> 🐾 Like most mice, Frankl was not good enough at mathematics to calculate how long it would take for things to go back to normal.

Frankl stood up and stretched mightily. "I say we've done plenty of thinking for today," he said. "Let's have some food and a good sleep, and worry about finding a solution tomorrow."

With mixed feelings the two friends parted company for the night. Each was pleased with having solved the riddle of the itching, yet both still wondered just how they would find a solution to the bird problem.

Frankl Explains:

Why it pays to keep asking "Why?"

Because many problems are complicated . . .

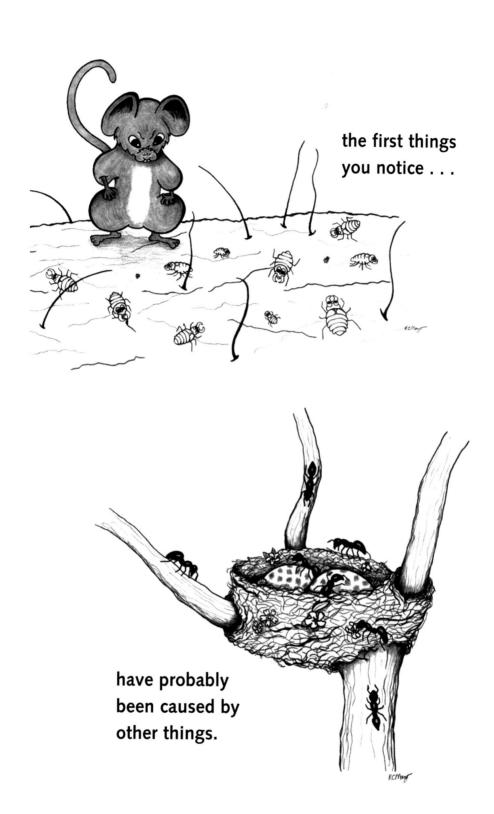

the first things you notice . . .

have probably been caused by other things.

PART THREE

11

Threats

WHILE BILLIBONK AND FRANKL were investigating bugs, birds, and ants, the rest of the elephant herd tried to ignore its misery—without much success.

"This itching is driving me mad!" Cody shouted, "and the more I itch the madder I'm getting at Billibonk!"

"What does Billibonk have to do with it?" Jawoody asked, wondering how Cody had concluded that their friend was at fault.

Cody sighed and tried to explain. "Billibonk was the first elephant to get this itch—it started with him. It's obvious that the rest of us must have caught the itch from him."

"I suppose you're right," Jawoody said, "though knowing whose fault it is doesn't make the itch go away." 👣

"Well, I don't think he should be allowed to get away with it. He's to blame, and he should be punished," Cody declared.

The rest of the herd began to murmur among themselves. In the past, they had occasionally punished

> 👣 Even though Jawoody was a thoughtful and experienced elephant, elephants are usually not good at spotting leaps of logic. If one elephant says that something is "obvious," other elephants usually feel uncomfortable about questioning him, even if they don't understand his thinking.

elephants who did something that hurt other members of the herd. Usually, though, these were minor offenses. The punishments were very small, too. Recently Cody accidentally sat on Honka's lunch, and had to be Honka's "slave-for-a-day." Not surprisingly, his duties consisted mostly of bringing the big elephant more food. But this itching problem was an altogether more serious matter.

Jawoody scratched her head with her trunk and asked, "How do you think Billibonk should be punished?"

Cody thought for a moment, and then announced, "Sending him out of the herd would teach him a lesson."

The other elephants gasped. "But he's your friend, Cody," one of them protested. "Would you really make him leave?"

Cody shifted his weight self-consciously. Billibonk *was* his best friend—but he had already blurted out his idea about punishment, and he didn't want to back down. "I *don't* want him to go," he said, "but if he does go, maybe the rest of us will finally stop itching."

Once again the others murmured among themselves. This time their heads were nodding in agreement. Cody had a good point—they all desperately wanted to stop the itching—and at the same time no one could deny that Cody still cared for Billibonk.

As they mulled over their dilemma, Billibonk himself wandered into the clearing and came over to join them. One by one, the elephants stopped talking. Some of them felt itchier just looking at him, and took that as further proof that Cody was right.

"Hi, everyone," Billibonk said hesitantly. "What's going on?"

Jawoody spoke up. "We've been talking, Billibonk. We want to get this itching business cleared up."

"So do I," Billibonk said eagerly. "And I think I'm about to find out what's causing it."

Jawoody cleared her throat. "Well, the rest of us are pretty sure that you're what's causing it," she said as kindly as she could.

Billibonk's mouth gaped. "Me?!" he said. "Why is it *my* fault?"

"You were the one who got the itch first," Cody reminded him. "It stands to reason that it's your fault."

Jawoody interrupted, hoping to find a way to calm everyone down. "If you really think you have an idea for stopping the itch, Billibonk, then help us. If you can stop it—let's say in the next three days—we won't have to punish you."

Billibonk's eyes grew wide, and his ears flapped in alarm. "Punish me?! What do you mean?"

"The herd has decided that if you can't fix this problem you've caused for us, then you'll have to go away until we've all stopped itching. It really is the best thing."

With that, the herd dispersed sadly, leaving Billibonk staring into space, his mind spinning in confusion.

12

Monkeys

BACK IN THE THORN PATCH, Frankl slept restlessly. His mind raced with thoughts of bugs, birds, and ants. When he did manage to doze off, he dreamed of trees crashing and eggs breaking.

Billibonk also spent a restless night. In between scratching, he worried ceaselessly about the herd's threat. How miserable he would be if the herd made him leave!

Waking early, he headed into the forest to find some breakfast. He decided to eat something a little different this morning, hoping that a change would help him think up a fast solution to the itching problem. As he approached a melon patch that he had noticed some days earlier, a dark shape suddenly swung down from the overhanging trees and landed on the path in front of him. "Chekup!" Billibonk said, recognizing his monkey acquaintance.

"Hey elephant!" Chekup said, scowling. He bothered with names only when talking with other monkeys. "*What* is going on?"

"What do you mean?" Billibonk asked.

"It's like this. We're getting tired of having our trees knocked over. When you swing through the jungle like we monkeys do, it's a little upsetting to reach for a tree and find it missing! Of course, we *are* superb athletes—but if we weren't, we would have a lot of injured monkeys around here. So how come you elephants are smashing our trees?"

This was almost too much for Billibonk—now even the monkeys were complaining to him. He struggled to stay calm. "Sorry, Chekup. We don't mean to cause any trouble. But lately we've all been very itchy, and sometimes when we scratch against a tree, the tree breaks."

"Itchy! You're smashing our trees because you're itchy?!" Chekup screeched.

"Like I say, I'm sorry about all the trouble. Frankl and I are trying to solve the itch problem, and, uh . . . it looks like it might take a while."

"Those mice love to take their time," Chekup snorted. "I wouldn't bother with them. Tell you what—leave things to me. In a couple of days, we monkeys will have everything all fixed up."

Billibonk's face lit up. He knew that although the monkeys could be unreliable at times, they were also very clever. And . . . he had only three days to solve the itching problem. "Can you really fix things, Chekup?" he asked hopefully.

"Sure!" the monkey said, strutting confidently. "Just stay away from our trees in the meantime." He scrambled up a nearby tree and disappeared into the jungle canopy, screeching and calling for the rest of his monkey friends.

Billibonk trotted on toward his melon patch, smiling and humming to himself. Despite his itch and his nervousness about being expelled from the herd, he decided that his prospects were looking better and better.

13

Ideas

AFTER EATING THEIR BREAKFASTS that morning, Billibonk and Frankl met again to talk about the problem of not enough birds. Billibonk decided not to tell Frankl about the herd's threat to expel him; Frankl was already trying his best, and Billibonk didn't want to put any more pressure on him. 🐾

The two friends talked about all the ways they could think of to get bug-birds back into the jungle. Frankl had never ventured outside Knith, and on the occasions Billibonk had traveled, he hadn't paid any attention to birds. So, they could hardly imagine finding birds from somewhere else. Nevertheless, when one bird flew by, they caught his attention and asked him if he and his friends would mind joining them on a search for new bug-birds.

> 🐾 While some animals think that extra pressure makes others think harder and better, Billibonk suspected that it just made others look for quicker answers, even if they were wrong.

The bird cackled. "You joke, right? Too busy. All birds busy. Chick time. Maybe later, when chicks big. Ask again in six months." And he flew off.

Billibonk and Frankl sighed, and then talked about maybe teaching other kinds of birds to eat the bugs. When they asked some birds about this, all of them said they would rather starve than eat bugs off an elephant.

By early afternoon, Frankl and Billibonk were exhausted from all the thinking and talking. They slumped side-by-side against a big rock, feeling like they hadn't gotten anywhere. 🐾

🐾 In fact, they had learned a great deal. They had discovered a bunch of ideas that did not work, and that was almost as valuable as finding ideas that did work.

"Well," Frankl finally said, "it's time to start thinking like a bird. Put me on that branch—I'm going to build a nest."

Billibonk raised one eyebrow in surprise as he lifted his friend and placed him carefully in the tree. "A nest—what good will *that* do?" he asked.

"I don't know yet," Frankl said. "It may do no good at all. On the other hand, it may help us think about the problem in a new way. Now send me up some grass."

Billibonk uprooted some clumps of grass with his trunk and handed them up to Frankl, who began arranging them into the shape of a bird nest. Of course, Frankl was used to building mouse nests, but this was a whole new skill. "How do birds manage this?" he wondered aloud, as pieces of his nest fell off the branch and floated to the jungle floor. He realized that bird nests and mouse nests were very different. Mouse nests are usually thrown together in cramped spaces, but a bird nest has to hold itself together on a branch.

He tried again, but this time a puff of wind knocked his nest off the branch. As it fell, the nest came apart in a flutter of grass. "Hey, Frankl," Billibonk said, pointing with his trunk to where the nest landed. "At least some parts of it stayed clumped together!"

Frankl squeaked in frustration and once more began rebuilding the nest with more grass from Billibonk. Every now and then, a bird flew

past and snickered at the sight, though to Frankl's eyes things were starting to come together quite nicely.

Suddenly the branch began shaking, and Frankl watched in horror as his nest tumbled to the ground. He peered down and then scowled. "Billibonk! What are you *doing*?!" he yelled.

The elephant looked up in surprise. He had been innocently rubbing his itchy back against the tree, and had no idea of the trouble he was creating. "Oh . . . ," he said, shame-faced. "Sorry, Frankl. Did you feel that?"

"*Feel* it?! I almost fell off this branch! My nest is ruined, thanks to you. I'll have to start all over again!"

"Why don't you stop, Frankl?" Billibonk said. "I don't think any bug-birds are going to come here and live in the nests you're making."

Frankl sputtered angrily. "I want to see what it's like to be a bird," he insisted, "and I don't think a bird would give up—"

He halted. An idea had popped into his head. He remembered Rork and Ella talking about having to rebuild a nest once. "That's it!" he yelled, jumping up and down excitedly. "That's it! Billibonk— you and I are going to be the champion itch-fixers in all the jungle. Get me down!"

14

Chicks

IT'S ALL SO SIMPLE, once you think about it!" Frankl explained to Billibonk. The elephant concentrated with all his might on what his friend was saying. "The important thing to remember is that it is the *chicks* who eat most of the bugs, not the grown-up birds. Rork said that during chick time, the grown-up birds spend all their time feeding bugs to the chicks."

"Yes, but don't you need grown-up birds to get chicks?" Billibonk asked.

"You said 'but' just now," Frankl pointed out. "Don't worry, though. I won't bite you—I'm too excited about my idea."

"OK, OK, tell me more," Billibonk said.

Frankl began: "You do need grown-up birds to get chicks, and we've got some: Rork and Ella. Any chicks they have will start eating bugs right away. The trick is to get Rork and Ella to have more than just two chicks. If they can have lots of chicks, then we can find a way to feed the bugs to the chicks until they're big enough to get on top of an elephant themselves and eat the bugs."

Frankl waited for Billibonk's reaction. "So, what do you think?"

"I think I'm having a hard time not saying 'but,'" Billibonk admitted.

"What part do you need me to explain?" Frankl asked.

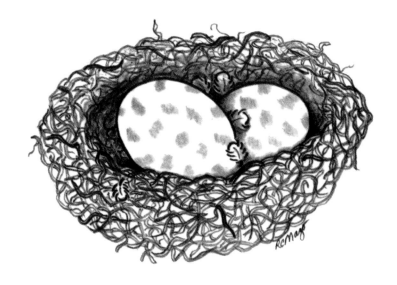

"Well, we've found out that the birds lay two eggs each season, and then they stop. Are they going to lay more eggs just because we want them to?"

"We already know they can lay more," Frankl said. "I remembered this when you knocked down my nest. Ella laid two eggs that broke when an elephant knocked over the tree; now she's about to lay two more. She keeps laying eggs until she has two to sit on, then she stops. If something happens to the two, she lays more. If we take her eggs away after she lays them, she'll probably lay another two. Then if we take those away, she'll lay more! Oh, I like this idea!" Frankl's whiskers twitched excitedly, and his eyes became even brighter than ever.

If the birds did this, they would be doing something called balancing—trying to get a balance between what they want and what they have. In this case, the birds want two eggs, and will keep working until they have them.

50

"How," Billibonk asked, "do we get all the eggs to hatch into chicks?"

"We have to find some other birds who will sit on them until they hatch. As long as the birds are about the same size as Rork and Ella, it won't matter to the eggs. Then when the chicks hatch, these foster-birds can feed them bugs."

"What if the foster-birds try to feed the chicks some other food, like berries?" Billibonk asked.

"I think each kind of bird eats one kind of food. I don't think bug-bird chicks will eat anything except bugs. Have you ever heard chicks yelling for food?" Billibonk nodded, remembering the noise. "If you were a bird with a couple of chicks in your nest screaming for bugs, I bet you'd get the bugs as fast as you could. These birds wouldn't have to eat the bugs themselves, just carry them back to the nest." 🐾

"Well . . . OK," Billibonk said, beginning to think that this plan could work. "I still have some questions, though. How long will it take for the plan to stop the itching?" He didn't want Frankl to know that he needed to solve the problem in three days.

> 🐾 Here's some more balancing: Bug-bird chicks want bugs, and when they haven't got any, they yell until some arrive. Adult birds want the chicks to be quiet. When the chicks yell, the adults bring them bugs until they stop.

"I don't know," Frankl replied. "It all depends on how long it takes for the chicks to hatch. Until then, Rork and Ella will still be the only bug-birds around. We'll have to ask *them*."

"That's another thing," Billibonk added. "Don't you think they'll complain if we keep taking their eggs? And what about the foster-birds? How can we be sure they'll want to help?"

"You're right—those *are* important questions. We'll have to ask Rork and Ella if they'll do it, and we'll have to find lots and lots of foster-birds to help."

"Let's start with Rork and Ella," Billibonk suggested.

Although they were both smiling and doing their best to appear optimistic, neither elephant nor mouse was confident the birds would agree to help. The approaching conversation would make or break their plan.

15

How Long?

FRANKL AND BILLIBONK found Rork collecting bugs from Honka's back. Once more Rork happily flew over to Billibonk's back to talk with Frankl. Ella had just laid her two new eggs and was busy sitting on them.

Frankl and Rork chatted for a time before Frankl mentioned his idea. "This elephant and I think we found a way to help get rid of the elephants' itching problem. If the plan works, the elephants will stop knocking down trees. The plan would mean a lot of work for you and Ella, so we want to share the work with you."

"Sure. Sure. Share," Rork replied.

Frankl explained the chick-hatching plan, pointing out all the reasons why he hoped it would work. Rork listened, snapping up bugs all the while.

When Frankl finished, there was a long silence as Rork considered the idea. "What do you think?" Frankl said at last.

"Like idea of getting lots of chicks fast. Whole flock by next season? Great. All Rork's and Ella's children! 👣 One thing wrong with plan. When take eggs, must smash nest, too."

> 👣 Like many animals, birds are very motivated to have lots of children, and often compete with one another to have the biggest families.

"Why?" Frankl asked. "Won't that mean even more work for you?"

"More work—no problem. Work what birds do now 'til chicks big. Work, work, work."

"Why do we have to smash the nests?"

"Just do. We build nest, have eggs. Always the same. No nest, no eggs."

"OK," Frankl said, appreciating the improvements on his ideas. "Should we try?"

"Talk with Ella. Tell you in morning."

"Wait," Frankl added. "How long do you sit on eggs before they hatch?"

"Not long—twenty days, then chicks out . . . . See you in morning," and Rork flew off.

Billibonk swung his head around to look at Frankl, his brow deeply furrowed. "Twenty days!" he cried in alarm.

"I'm sorry, Billibonk," Frankl said. "That's how long it takes. Once we start our plan, though, Ella will be laying eggs every couple of days. She has two eggs now, so that means in twenty days, the first chicks will hatch. Then there'll be a couple more chicks every couple of days after that."

Billibonk stammered, "That . . . that's too long!"

"This isn't a fast solution," Frankl admitted, "but it's a lot better than two or three years, don't you think?"

Billibonk snorted. Though he didn't want to seem ungrateful, he wondered how he was going to keep from getting thrown out by the herd. He also dreaded the thought of itching for another 20 days or even more. Things were beginning to look very, very bad.

He and Frankl walked back to the mouse's thorn patch in silence. Suddenly Chekup swung down from a branch and landed on the path in front of them. "Hi elephant," he said to Billibonk. "The anti-itch medicine is coming along nicely. It'll be ready tomorrow, early."

And with that, he leapt up, grabbed the branch again, and disappeared into the treetops.

"What was *that* all about?" Frankl asked.

"The monkeys are making something to fix our itch," Billibonk answered, a bit defensively. "Maybe it'll take a lot less than twenty days to work!"

"Will the medicine get rid of the bugs?" Frankl asked skeptically. "If it gets rid of the itch without getting rid of the bugs, it won't really fix the problem."

"You just don't understand!" Billibonk burst out. "I *have* to solve this problem—*fast*!" He snatched Frankl off the top of his head and set him down roughly on the ground. "I need some sleep; let's see how things go tomorrow." He stomped off back to the herd, wondering if anyone, anywhere really understood him.

Frankl looked after him sadly, then started trudging toward home. He was trying to be helpful, and he thought they had made wonderful progress that day. Yet clearly their plan just wasn't good enough for Billibonk. It occurred to Frankl that his friendship with Billibonk might be in danger, and his nose began to twitch with worry.

Frankl Explains:

Why blaming isn't helpful

Even though
blaming someone
else might make
you feel better . . .

it stops you
from talking
to each other . . .

when instead you could
be working together to
solve the problem.

PART FOUR

16

Monkey's Lotion

WHEN FRANKL WOKE the next morning, he set out immediately to learn about the "medicine" that Chekup and the other monkeys were mixing up for the elephants. As he scurried along the jungle paths to the elephant clearing, he saw that Ella was up early, too, breakfasting on the bugs on Honka's back.

Frankl hopped over to where Honka lay sleeping, and called up to Ella. "Hey, bird. How are you this morning?"

"Good. Good," Ella squawked back. "Rork's turn on eggs. My turn on elephant. Bugs taste best when pick your own!"

Frankl asked, "Did Rork talk with you about our plan?"

"Yes. Yes. We like idea. Get lots of chicks. Grow up fast. Soon have flock. Good. Good."

"Great!" Frankl said. "Now we have to find some other birds to help."

"No trouble. We help. Lots of birds can help. Now taking bugs to Rork. Then go talk to birds." She collected a few more bugs for her mate and flapped into the air.

"I hope she's right," Frankl thought to himself. He wasn't at all sure that finding foster-birds would be easy.

As he mulled this over, a gang of four monkeys bounded into the clearing and yelled, "Wake up, elephants! Time for a wash!"

All around the clearing, the elephants began opening their eyes sleepily. "What's going on?" Cody mumbled.

"Time to try our superfabulous anti-itching treatment," Chekup announced. "Come on, hurry, hurry. Follow us—the lotion won't come to *you*!"

Frankl had just enough time to scramble onto Billibonk's back as the elephants lumbered to their feet and set off after the monkeys down the path. Soon the whole crowd came to another clearing. In the center of the clearing stood a large tree stump, left there after a tree had fallen down. The monkeys had carved out much of the wood from the center, so that the stump formed a kind of large bowl.

At the urging of the monkeys, the elephants gathered around the stump and peered inside. The stump was filled with a murky liquid, which was dotted with chunks of fruit, floating on the surface.

"What is it?" Jawoody said, breathlessly.

"This is the anti-itch treatment," Chekup explained. "It's a lotion. We'll splash it on you."

> In truth, the monkeys didn't know how this lotion stopped itches. They did know it worked only when made in certain stumps. This is because these special stumps contain an oil that gets into the lotion. The oil stops itches in two ways. It makes skin taste very bad to bugs, so they stop biting. It also soothes the irritation caused by earlier bites.

"How did you make it?" Billibonk said suspiciously.

"Oh, that's a bit complicated," Chekup said. "It's something we monkeys have used for years. First, you get lots of juicy fruit and put it in the stump. Then you jump up and down on the fruit to make the juice all squish out. After a while the lotion gets all sticky, and that's when we put in on you. The special mix of fruits we use stops the itch."

Cody, who had complained the loudest about his itching, edged closer to the stump. "I'll try it," he said. At Chekup's instruction he sucked up a snozzleful  of the juice and squirted it over his back.

Chekup swung himself up onto Cody's back and with a large, leafy branch began to spread the lotion all over his elephant patient. Cody sighed contentedly.

>  **A snozzleful is half a trunkful.**

After a few minutes, when the herd saw that nothing strange happened to Cody, they all lined up for the treatment. Even Honka had the monkeys spread lotion on his back, claiming that it would help *prevent* him from getting itchy.

Billibonk and his friends were feeling fabulous. Their itching had quickly subsided. "Can you make more of this if the itch comes back?" Cody asked Chekup.

"Sure. We can do that. We'll get some ready for you now, just in case."

"Great!" the elephants trumpeted joyfully, and then they sauntered off to look for breakfast. Jawoody wandered over to Billibonk. "Well," she said, "looks like you've done it. This monkey lotion really works.

You won't have to leave the herd now."

Frankl, who was still sitting on Billibonk's back and was now having to clean sticky fruit juice from his fur, pricked up his ears. "Leave the herd?!" he thought to himself. "No wonder why Billibonk was in such a rush to find a cure. But this juice *can't* be the answer! I can still see bugs all over Billibonk's back. Maybe it makes the itch less noticeable, but it doesn't do anything about the *real* problem! It just makes the elephants think the problem is gone. And as long as they *think* the problem is gone, they won't do anything to solve it."

Frankl began cleaning his whiskers nervously. "I'm going to *have* to talk with Billibonk about this tomorrow," he decided to himself.

17

Foster-Birds

WHILE THE ELEPHANTS were enjoying their treatment, Ella had taken the bugs back to Rork. Then she took a tour of all the nests in her tree. A jungle is full of birds—one large tree can contain dozens of different nesting birds, along with other birds that don't have mates.

As she hopped from branch to branch visiting the nests, she talked with different birds about the elephants' itching problem. Many of the birds were already alarmed at the tree-smashing that had been going on. They were very interested in finding ways to stop elephants from using the trees to scratch. 🐾

Ella finally collected a group of birds who were willing to help hatch Ella's and Rork's eggs and raise the chicks. Some of these were birds who hadn't found

> 🐾 Some birds are most interested in helping other animals and making the jungle a better place to live. Others are mainly interested in making things better for themselves, thinking that if everyone does this, then the whole jungle will be better off. Knowing this about her neighbors, Ella explained how the chick-hatching plan would help the birds themselves and the jungle as a whole.

mates. Others weren't ready yet to lay their own eggs and wanted to practice chick-raising. Some were older birds who had stopped laying eggs of their own and wanted to help.

Ella arranged for two birds to take the eggs she had already laid, and set the birds to work building a nest near her own. She carefully explained the need to use elephant hairs in the nest building. Then she flew off to find Frankl, to tell him about her progress.

She finally found the mouse in the clearing where the elephants had been slathering on the new lotion. The herd had wandered off to look for breakfast, and Frankl was scurrying around the clearing, stopping occasionally to clean his whiskers, as mice often do when they're nervous.

"What's up, mouse? You worried?"

"Yes," Frankl admitted, grateful for the chance to talk about his concerns. "I think the elephants are in trouble." He told Ella about the monkeys' anti-itch treatment.

"What wrong with lotion?" Ella asked.

"After their wash, they feel happy. They don't itch so much. After a while, they'll be so used to using the lotion they'll never do anything to fix the real problem!"

"Sound like you need talk to elephants. Find one who smart."

"I know one who's smart," Frankl said, "but he's not very happy with me at the moment. He thinks the chick-rearing plan is going to take too long. And the other elephants are threatening to kick him out of the herd!"

"You talk anyway," Ella advised. "You help elephants lots. They know that. You talk. He listen."

"Thanks, Ella," Frankl said.

"No trouble. Hey, you help *me* now. How we move eggs from my nest to foster nest?"

"We'll have to carry them somehow."

"Bird not carry. Eggs too big. Mouse carry?"

"No. They're too big for us, too. The only animals I know who could carry eggs through trees are monkeys."

"Great," Ella said, always willing to work hard to get a job done. "You talk to elephant. I talk to monkey." She flew away, leaving Frankl wondering just what he was going to say to Billibonk.

18

The Trap

ELLA FOUND CHEKUP and his friend Jaks in the clearing, preparing a new anti-itch lotion for the elephants. They were stomping up and down in the stump, trampling the fruit that other monkeys had gathered.

Ella perched on the edge of the stump and called, "Hey monkeys."

"What do you want, bird?" Chekup asked rudely. "We're busy."

"Need help from monkeys. Need to move eggs."

"What for?" Chekup asked, stopping his stomping for a moment.

"Mouse's plan. Get more chicks. Help stop elephants scratching."

"We have our own plan, bird. Why should we help you?" Chekup said.

"Yeah . . . what's in it for us?" Jaks chimed in.

> 👣 Most monkeys think of themselves first and the jungle later.

The two monkeys had little interest in birds. Though they often met birds in the trees, they thought birds were slow-witted because of the way they spoke. They didn't bother talking with them for very long, so they never found out how smart birds really were.

Ella laughed. "You in trouble, monkey, and you not know it."

Chekup sneered at her. "Why's that?" he asked.

"How long you plan to keep making lotion?" Ella asked him. Ella, like most animals, knew that monkeys were famous for giving up on

projects when they got bored, or when something more interesting came along.

"I don't know," Chekup answered. He hadn't really thought about it. "When we get tired of it, I guess."

"Think again, monkey," Ella cackled. "You stop washing elephants, they start itching again. They get mad at you, they smash trees again. Bad, bad, bad."

Chekup and Jaks looked at each other. They could see how things could turn out just the way the bird said. Ella cackled on, "You in trap, now! Elephants used to have problem. Now monkey got it—got an elephant on his back!" 🐾

> 🐾 Often, when someone tries to help others, the others come to depend on that help. Helpers have to be careful how they help, so that others also learn how to take care of themselves.

"All right, all right," Chekup said grumpily. "Don't go on about it. What do you want us to do?"

"You keep making lotion. Make lotion 'til mouse say stop. Plus, help move eggs. Move two today. Again when I say. Not much work. Birds work much harder."

Chekup and Jaks nodded, although they weren't too happy about the plan. Chekup's sneer had turned into a scowl. He could see that the monkeys had no choice, and he was starting to suspect that Ella was smarter than he had thought.

"Come on, come on," Ella squawked. "One monkey come now. Move eggs."

"*You* go," Chekup muttered to Jaks. "I'll finish making the lotion."

Ella set off through the forest, flying from branch to branch as she led Jaks back to her nest.

The chick-hatching scheme was under way.

19

Herd Learning

EARLY AFTERNOON THE NEXT DAY, Frankl hurried over to the elephant clearing. The herd was slumbering in the midday heat. Frankl climbed up into a tree, where he could see all the elephants. Billibonk was the first elephant to wake. Instead of hoisting himself to his feet, however, Billibonk cocked his head to one side and stared across the clearing. His trunk began to wrinkle up with disgust. A few flies were beginning to buzz around him.

The rest of the herd woke in a similar manner. Eyes widened, trunks curled, and each elephant in turn cried, "What's that dreadful smell?" Eventually Jawoody suggested that it might be the smell of fruit rotting in the jungle heat. The herd squinted at each other, some of them wondering who to blame.

Finally Billibonk said, "We need to talk about this monkey lotion. I don't think it's the answer to our itch."

"But it works—it stops the itching," Jawoody protested.

"Only for a while—I'm already starting to itch again," Billibonk said.

"My itch is worse now than it's ever been," said Cody. 🐾

> 🐾 Cody was right. The taste of the lotion had stopped the bugs from biting, without making them go away. As the lotion wore off, the bugs began biting again, only now they were hungrier, and so they bit harder.

"Do you know what's making us itch?" Billibonk asked the herd.

"Not being big enough," Honka suggested. The others scowled at him irritably.

"No—size isn't the issue," Cody said. "I think we started itching because we didn't have the monkey lotion."

"You know," Billibonk said. "I've been thinking about this. We weren't itchy a month ago, or a year ago, and we didn't have the monkey lotion then. And Honka, you weren't itchy when you were smaller. So it must be something else."

"What could it be, then?" Jawoody asked.

"Well," Billibonk replied. "I think it's bugs. Birds normally eat them off us, and they haven't been doing that lately. It's the bugs that make us itchy."

To Billibonk's surprise, Cody responded, "I think you're right. I've noticed birds riding on us before, and I've often wondered what they were doing."

Billibonk explained further: "The good news is that the birds are going to fix the problem themselves. It's just going to take a while— maybe twenty or thirty days."

"Well then," Honka announced. "We could just use the monkey lotion until the birds fix the problem." The rest of the herd nodded their heads slowly, taking care to keep their trunks extended to where they could find fresh air.

"That's a great idea!" Billibonk said. "We should stop using the lotion as soon as possible, though. It makes us feel good, but then it starts to stink. And, it doesn't really solve the itch problem—it just makes it *seem* like the problem is gone."

"That's true," Jawoody admitted. "Let's make some rules about the monkey lotion. One rule is: We put it on at night, then wash it off in the morning."

"And," Billibonk added, "no monkey lotion for any elephant who's not itchy. Honka, you don't need any, and you can be in charge of making sure others who aren't itchy don't use it. That way, there will always be some in the herd who don't smell. Otherwise, we might start getting used to this stink."

Honka was delighted to be given an important task because of his great size. "Sure," he agreed, trying not to sound too eager.

The elephants clambered to their feet and headed quickly for the river to wash. They took care not to swing their trunks in the usual elephant manner, for fear that they might catch too big a whiff of themselves.

Billibonk lingered in the clearing, enjoying the quiet. All of a sudden, Frankl came scrambling down from his tree, and scampered across the clearing to greet him. "Billibonk," Frankl said, "sometimes you elephants are amazing. Just when I want to give up on you, you get really smart!"

Billibonk blushed shyly. "Thanks, Frankl!" he said. "Do you know what I've discovered? It's really hard to think straight when you've got a problem, even though that's what you need to do most. I'm sorry if I was cranky with you these last few days."

"That's OK," Frankl reassured him. "That's just part of being friends."

20

The Last "Why"

AFTER A FEW MONTHS HAD PASSED, the elephant clearing was a much happier place than before. The trees surrounding the clearing rang with the clamor of bug-bird chicks yelling "More bugs! More bugs!" Elephants relaxed beneath the trees, making it easy for the foster-birds to collect bugs from their backs. With Rork's coaching, the foster-birds could now scoop up three bugs and fly back to the nest without accidentally swallowing or dropping any. The bug population was returning to normal—happy news for the elephant herd.

One morning, Rork noticed Frankl hopping into the clearing. The bird swooped down for a chat. "Hi Rork!" Frankl said. "How are things?"

"Great. Great. Chicks get big, fat. Sound good, don't you think?"

"They certainly are loud," the mouse agreed. Baby birds were much louder than any mouse baby he had heard. "Does the noise bother the foster-birds?" he asked.

"No. No. Birds all same. Chicks keep yelling, birds keep feeding. When chicks feed themselves, they stop yelling. Means birds make sure chicks grow up fast!"

Across the clearing, Billibonk saw Rork talking and wondered if he was with Frankl. He wandered over to join them, Ella balanced on his back. Because of her hard work producing eggs, the herd had decided that she had the right to eat bugs from any elephant.

"Hey elephant," Rork greeted Billibonk. "How's itch?"

"I'm feeling great, thank you!" Billibonk answered. "So is the whole herd." Rork flapped his wings, pleased. Billibonk turned to Frankl. "I've been wondering about something," he said. "You told me a while ago that you normally ask 'why' five times. We asked it only four times—Why are the elephants itching? Why are there too many bugs all of a sudden? Why did birds leave the forest? Why did ants invade the bird nests?—Do you think we could learn anything from asking 'why' again?"

"Well, let's try it," Frankl said. He hopped closer to the birds and asked, "Why did the birds start to use herbs in their nests instead of elephant hairs?"

"Maybe liked the smell?" Rork shrugged.

"No. No," Ella interrupted. "Started a while ago. Mice fancy themselves up. Put flowers and herbs on head, all over backs. Walk around smelling pretty. Birds like it—try it themselves."

"That right!" Rork confirmed, suddenly remembering the mice parading around in their new finery. "Elephants and mice all went to a party—something about Thorn Monsters."

Billibonk blushed furiously. The year before, the elephants, mice, and monkeys had tried to trick each other, with embarrassing results for everyone. Elephants have excellent memories. Try as he might, Billibonk would never forget that time. Frankl, too, blushed to the ends of his whiskers.

Suddenly they were interrupted by loud squawking. They all looked up to find the source of the noise. Four adult bug-birds flew down and landed on Billibonk's back. "My sons! My sons!" Ella screeched, flapping her wings excitedly. "Rork, come see. Boys are back!"

Frankl and Billibonk smiled at the bug-bird reunion. Rork's and

Ella's sons were introducing their mates to their parents, who assured them that there were plenty of elephants to go around.

"Well," Frankl said to Billibonk. "It looks like the trees will be safe from you elephants for a while." Billibonk grinned. "Just stay away from those flowers and herbs," Frankl added. He patted Billibonk's trunk. "You smell just fine the way you are."

Billibonk chuckled. "You know," he said. "I was feeling really clever until we asked that last 'why.' It seems that just when I start thinking I'm brilliant, something happens that makes me find out I'm not."

Frankl nodded. "I think that happens to everyone who wants to learn. It certainly happens to me. Remember, though—it didn't help you to solve the problem when the other elephants were blaming you, so I don't think blaming yourself will help either. That Thorn Monster trick did turn out to be a big mistake. Yet look how much we learned because of it."

Billibonk thought for a while. "So are you saying that mistakes are good?" he asked.

"I'm not saying you should go out of your way to make them," Frankl clarified. "Both of us will make plenty without even trying. What we should do is learn from them when we can."

"Do you know what?" Billibonk announced. "I'm actually looking forward to my next problem." He quickly added, "I just hope the next one isn't an itch!"

Why it takes hard work to find solutions that last

Because it's hard to live with a problem . . .

you might be tempted
to just treat the symptom . . .

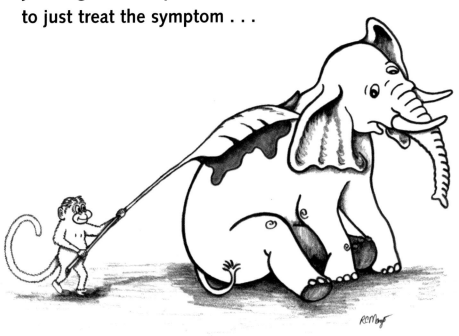

instead of waiting for the
real solution to work.

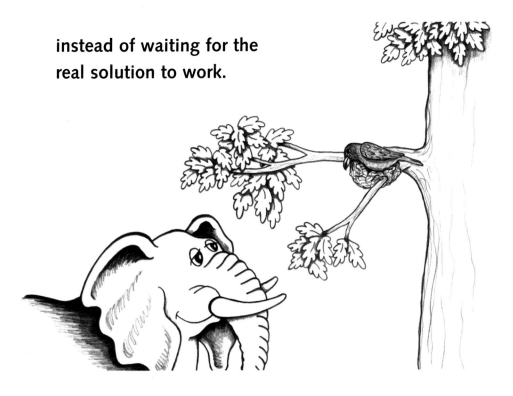

Acknowledgments

THIS IS THE SECOND STORY I have written about Billibonk's and Frankl's adventures, and it seemed much easier to do than the first, *Billibonk and the Thorn Patch*. Some things, like thinking of names for characters and a title for the book, were just as difficult the second time around. The main difference seems to be that all the people involved in the book keep getting better at what they do and in how they work with each other.

As with the first book, I've been helped enormously by my family: my children, Alex and Nick, and my wife Debbie. Each of them has contributed wonderful ideas that have been built into the story and the design of the book. Laurie Johnson and Kellie Wardman O'Reilly at Pegasus Communications have again been spectacular in making sure that the story was polished and the best it could be. And again, Robin Mazo has contributed brilliant illustrations.

Occasionally, a friend who had read *Billibonk and the Thorn Patch* would ask me if any of the details about life in the jungle of Knith were true. I've taken the approach that it is most important to make the principles true, even if the details are fantasy. It is nice, though, when bits of reality can be built into the story, and a number of people have helped me to do this with the book you are holding. Possible treatments for itches were suggested to me by my father-in-law, Jack Smith, and my lovely friend Linda Hull, along with her workmates at Morrison's Pharmacy. New Zealand's Department of Conservation is a world leader in the preservation of endangered birds. Frankl's chick-hatching scheme is based on their work to protect the New Zealand Black Robin, which several years ago held the title of the world's most endangered bird.

The adventures of Billibonk and Frankl are based on principles and concepts from the literature on organizational learning. After a while, it becomes hard to remember where I first came across a particular idea, so it can be difficult to give credit where it is due. I can recall that I was greatly helped with this story by the work of the following people: Rick Ross, who has explained the use of "The Five Whys"; Peter Senge, with his description of the "Shifting the Burden" systems archetype; Daniel Kim, who has worked closely with the complexities of problem articulation; Chris Argyris and Bill Isaacs, who have done so much on dialogue; David Reynolds, with his common sense about feelings; and Marilyn Paul, who has explained the false sense of progress that comes from blaming.

It is challenging, exciting, and fun to write stories like this one. My thanks go to all those mentioned above, who made this book possible.

Phil Ramsey

Other Titles by Pegasus

The Natural Step: A Framework for Achieving Sustainability in Our Organizations

Anxiety in the Workplace: Using Systems Thinking to Deepen Understanding

The Soul of Corporate Leadership: Guidelines for Values-Centered Governance

Pegasus Communications, Inc. is dedicated to helping organizations soar to new heights of excellence. By providing the forum and resources, Pegasus helps managers articulate, explore, and understand the challenges they face in the complex, changing business world. For information about *The Systems Thinker*™ Newsletter, the annual *Systems Thinking in Action*™ Conference, the *Power of Systems Thinking*™ Conference, or other publications that are part of *The Organizational Learning Resource Library*™ Catalog, contact:

Pegasus Communications, Inc.
One Moody Street
Waltham, MA 02154-5339
Phone: (617) 398-9700   Fax: (617) 894-7026
www.pegasuscom.com